A Christmas Cookie Exchange

Sheri Wall
Illustrated by Ilona Stuijt

Printed in the United States of America
First Printing, 2017
ISBN-13: 978-1979568234

Children often struggle with feelings of inadequacy, resentment, and envy, especially during the holidays.

A CHRISTMAS COOKIE EXCHANGE
is a sweet story that can help reinforce the importance of nurturing positive character traits and avoiding unfounded comparisons.

My hope is that adults too can benefit from this thoughtful reminder.

I truly appreciate the love and support of my family and friends.

Here's to contentment and kindness and the celebration of the season.

Joy to all, Sheri Wall

December, that magical
time of the year,
when good friends and families
spread love and good cheer.

With invitations delivered,
the tree and halls trimmed,
it's time for a party.
Let the festivities begin!

The doorbell sings sharply.
Its voice holds a note,
as excited guests enter,
bundled warm in wool coats.

Hugs, laughter, bright smiles
are in view all around.
Exchanged are the packages.
Bows drop to the ground.

The feast looks extravagant,
and smells so divine.
There are too many choices
down the long buffet line.

Now at the dessert table,
silver trays take their places.
Amongst treats and goodies,
poinsettias fill vases.

Relaxing on lace sheets,
in tidy, neat rows,
the cookies look special,
and strike a fine pose.

Except for one cookie,
a plump disc named Phil.
He sighs with deep sadness,
but remains very still.

"Why can't I be fancy,
with sprinkles and icing,
or chocolate, or almonds,
or cinnamon spicing?

If only, if only,
someone would choose me,
they'd know that inside,
I'm sweet as can be."

*Sugar is so shapely,
in bright colors and piping.
Visitors compliment her,
and commence with their swiping.*

And Phil sighs...

"Why can't I be fancy,
with sprinkles and icing,
or chocolate, or almonds,
or cinnamon spicing?

If only, if only,
someone would choose me,
they'd know that inside,
I'm sweet as can be."

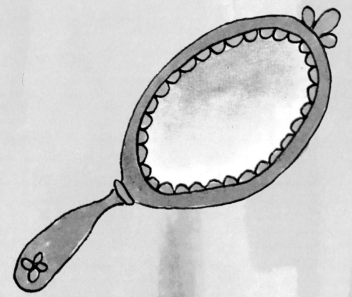

Then Phil slowly slides over
to make room for "the Man."
A ginger, he's spicy,
and has many fans.

And Phil sighs...

"Why can't I be fancy,
with sprinkles and icing,
or chocolate, or almonds,
or cinnamon spicing?

If only, if only,
someone would choose me,
they'd know that inside,
I'm sweet as can be."

Phil sees Cocoa beside him,
with her shiny, rich cape.
She entices the grazers,
and makes her escape.

And Phil sighs...

"Why can't I be fancy,
with sprinkles and icing,
or chocolate, or almonds,
or cinnamon spicing?

If only, if only,
someone would choose me,
they'd know that inside,
I'm sweet as can be."

Now Skip, round and nutty,
has such defined abs.
Although some must avoid him,
he gets many grabs.

And Phil sighs...

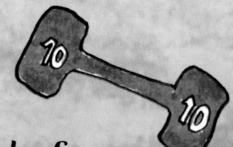

"Why can't I be fancy,
with sprinkles and icing,
or chocolate, or almonds,
or cinnamon spicing?

If only, if only,
someone would choose me,
they'd know that inside,
I'm sweet as can be."

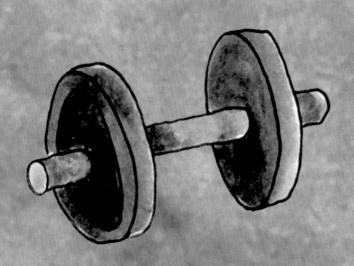

As replacements come warmly,
to reside next to Phil,
they notice his sadness,
and convey him goodwill.

"Dear Phil, we've been listening,
to your envious cries.
Stay cool now, don't crumble,
as we empathize.

We're dressed for the party,
as Christmas ensues,
but when it's all over,
and decorations we lose,

we then must rely on,
ingredients tested and true.
We're treasured as tasteful,
even fruitful like you."

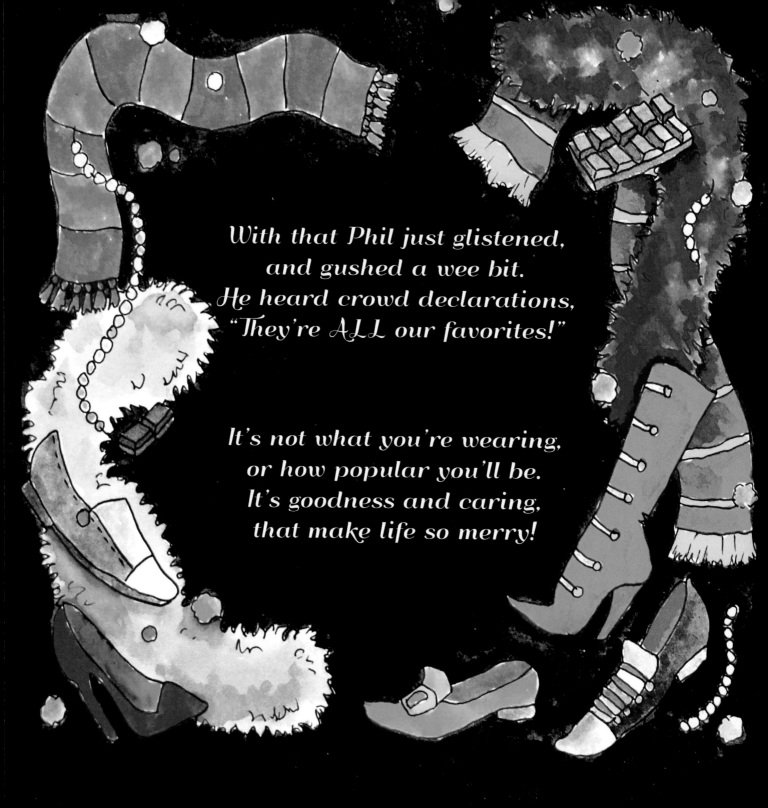

With that Phil just glistened,
and gushed a wee bit.
He heard crowd declarations,
"They're ALL our favorites!"

It's not what you're wearing,
or how popular you'll be.
It's goodness and caring,
that make life so merry!

The End

Sheri Wall is a wife and mother of two boys
residing in Central Texas.

With prompting from her husband,
she decided to begin authoring children's books.

Sheri then established her niche,
A Matter of Rhyme, which celebrates rhythmic
reading aloud as a fun, essential learning tool.

In addition to writing and rhyming,
Sheri enjoys cooking, eating, decorating,
bargain hunting and being active.
She can be reached at amatterofrhyme.com.

See more of Ilona Stuijt's illustrations and creative
works at drawnwithlove.weebly.com.

Made in the USA
Lexington, KY
02 December 2018